The KOALA Who Could

For my wonderful, brilliant,
adventureful dad . . . the most
CAN-DO Kevin I know. — R.B.

For Remi and Jack — J.F.

Text copyright © 2017 by Rachel Bright
Illustrations copyright © 2017 by Jim Field
First published in the United Kingdom in 2017
by Orchard Books London

Library of Congress catalog card number: 2016050758

ISBN 978-1-338-13908-2

10 9 8 7 6 5 4 3 2 1   17 18 19 20 21

Printed in China   38
First edition, November 2017

Rachel Bright

Jim Field

The KOaLa Who Could

Scholastic Press • New York

In a wonderful place,

where the day was just dawning

and the breezes blew soft

on a warm golden morning,

In a place where the creatures
ran wild and played free . . .
a koala called Kevin
clung to a tree.

A nicer gray fellow
you never would meet,
As SOFT as a SOFT THING
from ear tufts to feet.

His favorite way
to relax in the sun
Was to cling and to nap
and to munch a leaf-bun.

And after all this,
well, he'd need a nice rest.

Yes, Kevin liked sticking
to what he knew best.

You see, high up was safe since he liked a slow pace,
While the ground down below seemed a frightening place.

TOO FAST
and TOO LOUD
and TOO BIG
and TOO STRANGE.

Nope. Kevin preferred not to move, or to change.

So he clung to his tree
as he knew what to do,
And was never too keen
to try anything new.

So when Wombat stopped by
and shouted one day,
"HEY, KEVIN! Why don't you
come down here and play?"

"Um . . . I think," he replied,
"I should stay on my plant.
I'm busy right now . . .
No. I'm sorry. I can't."

"WHY NOT?" cried the roos,
with a SUPER loud cheer.
"YES, WHY?" called the dingoes.

"THERE'S NOTHING TO FEAR!"

But Kevin, who'd never
been one to act fast,
Said, "I've clinging to do.
But it's nice that you asked."

As Kevin sat watching
them chatter and share,
A part of him wished
he could join in down there.

But he knew he'd miss home
. . . it was dark and *SO* late.

The whole thing was risky.
Adventure could wait.

Whatever the invite,
he'd always say **NO**.
Oh dear, it seemed Kevin . . .

. . . just couldn't let go.

So his life
was the same,
no matter the day.

The weeks
came and went, and the
months rolled away.

And Kevin stayed still
while the world
moved around,

Until he

awoke to a

WORRYING sound . . . .

TAP TAP TAP

TAP TAPPITY TAP

the sound went.

Well . . . this was a blow!

"UN-CLING!" the crowd called, which had gathered below.

"Leap and we'll catch you! Just let yourself go!"

But Kevin was scared.

"Let go?
NO, I shan't!"

"I won't!"

shouted Kevin,

"Oh dear, **I JUST**. . .

WHOOOOOOMPF!

Down came the tree
and with it was bringing . . .
Crash and a **WALLOP** . . .
a Kevin still clinging!

Kevin, he carefully opened one eye

and looked up at the love staring down from the sky.

Then one paw by one paw, he loosened his hold . . .

He felt SPRINGY and

LIGHT and

HAPPY and

BOLD!

The worst he could think of had now come to pass
and he was JUST FINE. Why, he felt quite first-class!
So when Wombat leaned over and held his paw out,
Kevin no longer felt worry or doubt . . .

When Dingo asked, "Now will you come out to play?"

The crowd all joined in with a "what-do-you-say?"

And even though this wasn't part of his plan,

Kevin replied, "Yes! I think that . . .

I CAN.

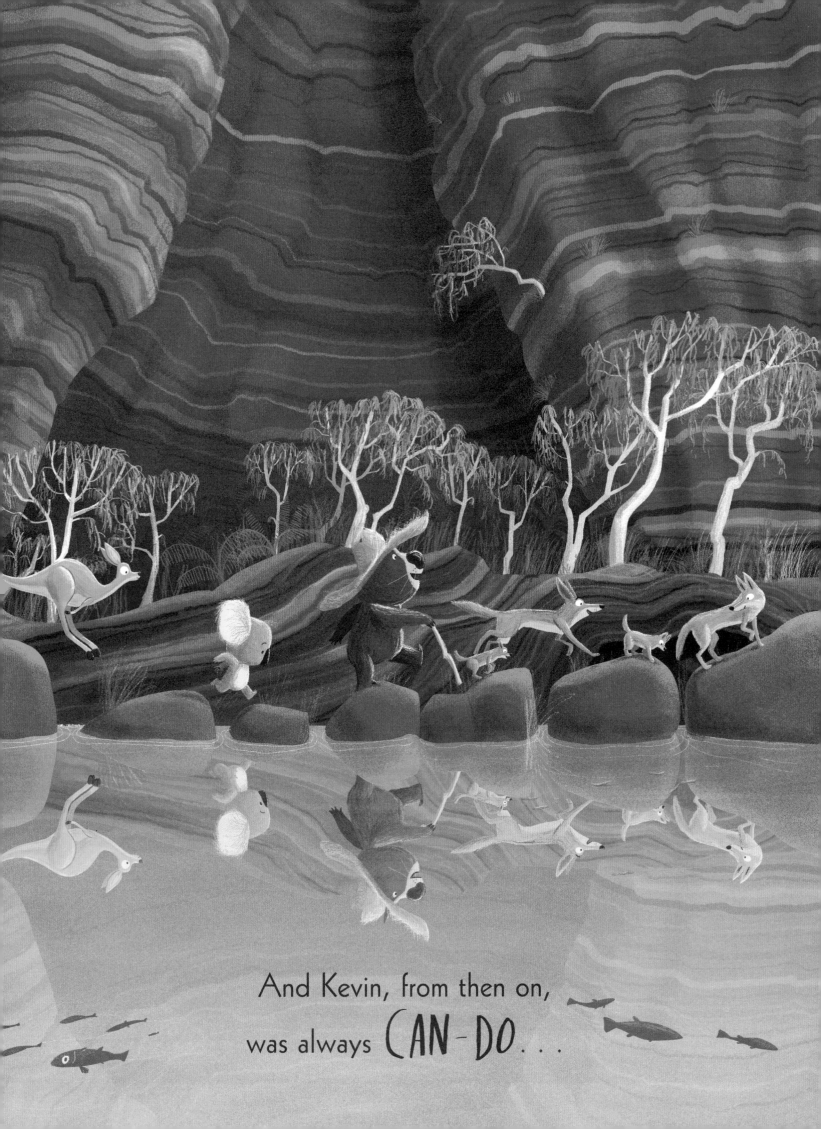

And Kevin, from then on,
was always CAN-DO . . .

Because life can be GREAT
when you try something
NEW!